Flower
Friend

Flower Friend

SARA HAJIPOURI

DEDICATION

This book is honored to my dad
Who raised me to follow my dreams
And showed me the beauty in everything
And to my sister
Who stood by me knowing
Someday I'd reach the stars

I want to express my utmost gratitude for your choice in reading my official debut poetry collection. Within its pages, you'll find a world where imagination runs free and where my ideas, thoughts, and stories come to life.

This collection began as a simple journal over two years ago, a creative outlet to calm my mind during a time when everything seemed uncertain and lost. I made a promise to myself to write just one poem a day, but that quickly grew into a collection of over 300 poems in a matter of months. I realized that the words I'd written to feel understood could have the same effect on others, becoming a source of comfort and companionship. While I may not have always felt like a friend to myself, my words somehow filled that void, and I hope they can do the same for you.

Having poured my soul into this collection, my greatest hope is that you discover your 'flower friend' somewhere along this book. Someone who will always be there for you, valuing your soul, guiding you through the darkness towards a path adorned with stars, and supporting the dreams that your heart creates. Perhaps the ultimate flower friend is yourself—deserving of more love from both the world and from within you. But if by chance you haven't found your flower friend by the book's end, let this collection, let my words, be there for you, and become your flower friend.

So, pour yourself a cup of tea, put on your favorite playlist, and as you gently descend into my poetry, I hope you're able to find yourself somewhere within its lines.

Gentle wishes,

TABLE OF CONTENTS

/ flower friend /

Blooming your perfect petals
Reaching to the sky
You are you
Leaning towards the sun
I wish to be you, my friend
Color so vibrant
Like a sunset sitting in the clouds
Hiding the dark, springing out light
Their eyes on your beauty
You don't notice, my flower
Why can't I be you?
The stars in your eyes
Bring the planets to you
Surrounding yourself
But you never knew
Oh, why can't I be you?
Flower friend
Why can't I be you?

Lost in the Clouds

/ fighting for you /

I once had a dream
I was somebody to me

/ 23 /

24
I'm too old
Have you not decided
What you're doing with your life?
Living in only deep thoughts
Of sunshines all the time
Have you not figured out
How to reach your dreams?
Become an adult it seems
Part of a dying society
Living in agony
If I listen to what they speak
I should've been a millionaire
By the age of 23

/ unwritten dream /

A reflection I see
Of someone that's not me
Of someone I could be
Someone living in my unwritten dream

/ chance /

Will I ever reach that mountain peak?
The ones in stories and songs
The ones where you only get there
With passions that seemed to take too long
But give me a chance
To prove that I can work my ankles to the moon
To prove how what I dream
Is what I will see soon
Just please, just this once
Appear a clover on my head
So that luck would finally, oh finally
Give me a chance

/ i'll ask myself again tomorrow /

I want to be someone more than I was yesterday
Is that too much to ask of myself?

/ *in the day* /

She thought she missed her chance
She lives counting stars in the day

/ *no* /

I've said "no"
To myself
For far too long
I've sadly forgotten
Who I wanted to become

/ reality /

I cry myself every night to sleep
Not because I want to
But because I must
Because dreams are more lovely
Than the reality I was told to trust

/ years in forever /

A forever years out of reach
I wonder if the dream we hold on to
Is just a feeling

/ *wishing on you* /

"How come when we wish on
a star, it never seems to come
true? It hurts my heart to
know this"

"Maybe the stars keep our
wishes until we need them
most"

"*…I never knew*"

/ so instead you watched the moon /

I watched you watch the sun
You wanted to be someone

/ so instead you watched the moon /

/ *my fault* /

I can't help but think
It's my own fault
That I'm this way

/ *fix you* /

I broke my own heart
It shattered when I stepped on it
It wasn't on purpose, but I don't think it knows
I'm sorry my heart, to fix you
What do I do?

/ to be me /

I do want to dream
But what's so difficult
In being the me
I want to see
A peaceful bird
Amongst a scattered galaxy
I just want to be me

/ *thereafter* /

Sweet glimpse of your light
Disappears too often
You want to be so much more
You have so much to offer
Eating away at you
That one moment you're after
That one moment where
Your light is permanent thereafter

/ *this is the past life we dreamt of* /

"I miss my past life. I had a
life in the clouds, my heart
danced with the flowers, my
beautiful mind saw
everything as a dream. I
never thought it would have
to end"

"What happened?"

"I grew older…that's what
happened"

/ pretending the clock doesn't tick /

I can't hope and think
Letting time move on
Pretending the clock doesn't tick
Pretending everyone's
Just standing still
Every day
The
Same
Walking to the mirror
Reflecting on my daily mistakes
Someone stares back
Someone I don't recognize
Someone I can't bear to face
Grey hair, wrinkles form a frown
Eyes who've lost their soul
I wish I hadn't let time move on
Leaving me so alone
I wish I had another second
To never let you go
I wish
I grabbed your hand
That day
I once told myself to never let go

/ *pause* /

I shut my eyes so tight
To where I can see the stars
The only way I know on
How to stop time

/ fate /

It would be easier
To let the stars decide my fate

/ beauty in me /

It's hard to admit
How the real beauty of this world
I can't see
The hidden serendipities
Their whimsical dreams
Maybe the reason
Is pure ignorance
On how I can't first see
The beauty
In me

/ *work without love* /

I just need time to cherish
And find my lost soul

/ *my voice* /

I whistled a tune in the wind
To find my voice again
But the wind took it
To a different dimension

/ *such things* /

I wonder sometimes
If happiness is something
I can achieve
Or am I just delusional
To think of such things

/ *ballerina: part i* /

A ballerina
I dance with words
But there will be a day
My ankles won't hold me anymore
And on that day
My soul stops dancing too

/ before i could /

So far from my dream
My age will soon catch up
Before I can ever reach
What I cry for, it seems

/ *alone* /

I didn't know what it felt like to be alone
Until I saw the deserted moon in the night
Or the broken butterfly left behind
Or how every autumn leaf
Never got a chance to say goodbye
But nothing compares to what it feels like
To be so alone
In your own mind

/ *waited* /

I woke up with a headache
Put the covers on my head
Waited until the sun
Went to bed

/ i really do /

I want to be happy
I really do
It's just so hard
To be something so new

/ *it's better this way* /

I just want to be a streetlight
At least then I'd be making a difference knowing
Someone will never have to walk alone in the dark

/ wishes /

I'm stuck in a dangerous loop
Of wishes and misses

/ *mine* /

The anger I feel
The anger that resides
For something so useless
Not worth my time
In my heart of all places
Why does it have to be mine?

/ *world of smiles* /

I can't fake a smile
Trust me
I've tried

/ in memories /

Good things don't last
Every memory
Is a broken thing from the past
All the good things
We've hoped to be
Will someday break us
In memories

/ *happy moments fade away* /

"I was happy today…"

"*Was?* Are you not anymore?"

"No, not anymore…because I
know that happy moments don't
last too long"

"Maybe happy moments aren't
supposed to last long. Maybe
we're meant to let them go, so
they can come back to us again.
I know if we hold on too long,
happy moments tend to fade
away…"

/ former times /

Don't let me fall
Into the blue skies of yesterday

/ *arguing with memories* /

I'd like my memories to stay memories
Not have them argue with me
As I desperately hold on to the present

/ what could /

The more I think
The more my head hurts
Since every day is spent
Thinking of what could be

/ so close /

The felicity I cannot have
But, I wish it weren't so

/ beautiful road /

Why is my path so delicately broken?
I can't seem to stay on track
When all the cars follow each other
On a neat and beautiful path
I'm stuck in the passenger seat
Of a car that wants to take the gravel road

/ *should i have said that* /

Even if I'm right, or wrong, or neither
The truth I wish I knew
As common as it is
Not a day can go by
Before the guilt wanders in
Leaving me trying to find
The reason I'm like this

/ ballerina: part ii /

My world breaks too soon
And the audience, they stare for me to move
Eventually my shoes
Are given to someone new
Them dancing with words
My heart finally breaks
Though it never wanted to

/ early morning sadness /

I hardly wake up happy
Sunlight has no meaning
Daunting dreams of the future
Are all I worry

/ *care* /

Sometimes
There are moments
When I care too much
And other times
Not enough

/ stars eventually fade /

I was there
Just this once
Could you be there for me too?

/ *not today* /

The sun isn't for me today
For someone else
It's shining bright

/ unlike me /

Like a small ant among butterflies
I longed to be flying with them

/ maybe kindness is a superpower /

Too kind, I let them take the world
I let them for so long
I don't know if I could
Ever get it back

/ *they want me to be* /

I have this idea
If they're happy, I'm happy
This false perception
A gift from society
That prevents me from being me
They pull me to their problems
Into *their* reality
This false perception
A gift from society
That prevents me
From being

/ remember /

The world is more broken
Than I remember

/ *angel in the way* /

You told me that I was your light
But I only saw you in the way
You pushed me towards the waves
But I wanted to push you away
The loving smile you gave every day
Made me turn away
And the heart you gave for me to hold
Could easily be let go today
I wanted it all, the unrealistic dreams
But your caution brought me pain
I hated how you stopped me
In order not to prevail
An angel in the way
I couldn't cross the tracks
Because you might have saved me
Before the nightmare, perhaps

/ i'm sorry /

I'm sorry for hurting you
I was naïve on what you were going through

/ stormy weather /

People like to stare
I know, since it's not common
For a cloud to follow me
Dark, only I can hear the
Thunder and only I
Can see the lightning

/ and i'll say this a thousand more times /

"If every person shared
compassion,
understanding, and
honesty with one
another, I don't see how
this world wouldn't be a
perfect place"

/ *never yours* /

Society tells you
This world was never
Yours to keep

/ left behind /

Scared to a wither
Everyone's running to make a mark
Painting the sky with a broken paint brush
Gluing the shattered glass, they've been hurt before
Teaching the lessons of the boundless words
So, they will not be the one forgotten
The one that disappears from memories
The one that left without an eternity

/ i can't /

Pushed around
They tell me what to do
I can't, I can't
My words shoved down
They show no respect
They get what they want
At the cost of my esteem
I allow this madness
My sadness allows this pain
I could tell them off
But at the cost of my dignity
I could show a frown
But at the cost of my name
There is no way to win
If I want respect
I must settle for this

/ right /

The good always wins, right?
Please, please tell me
That the good always wins

/ heartless /

In an instant, they could fade
Letting you linger in your thoughts
Of what you did wrong
Guilt, for nothing
·In an instant
They could bring sadness
In an instant
They could be heartless

/ the subtle darkness /

Life isn't fair
And no matter how hard I try to change it so
I fall deeper into the abyss
I'm being blinded by the subtle darkness
And you have no idea
How much I hate it

/ infinite world /

You had the world in your hands
But you wanted more
The moon, the stars, the planets
But you still wanted more
You wanted the galaxy
An infinite world

/ why can't it be you /

Why was I the one to make you happy?
Why couldn't you do the same for me?

/ marshmallow sweater /

That's what you thought
And at that time
I longed not to believe your words

/ goodbye friend /

"Is this how
friendships end? One
says goodbye and the
other gets left
behind?"

"You left. *You left me.*
I was always there,
but you saw me as
just a shadow in your
world. I'm the one
who should say
goodbye"

/ fairytale /

This fairytale world
You took for yourself
Leaving me with the wolf
And the wicked witch of the west

/ *riddance* /

When you stepped out that door
Did you think of me?
Did you care to dream
Who I would be?

/ *maybe* /

Maybe if the world could be you
They wouldn't be so mean
To a heart that's still healing

/ you left before me /

Crinkled skin, I can hardly open my eyes
My home I see through a frosted sheet
And my hands can't even lift me onto my feet
Although it takes almost an eternity
I'll never give up voluntarily
Kindly I walk through the quiet house
His face I can no longer pronounce
Leaving another flower on his empty armchair
The one I used to love
My sweet sweet dear

/ you left before me /

/ past the horizon /

Where can I go from here?
Time moves so slowly
Everyday heartaches
Staring out the window
Trees block my view of
The possible horizon

/ *little petals* /

I plucked them one by one
The little petals
Each flower gave a wince
Then disheartenly cried
Falling to the earth

/ *tears* /

My lonely friend
The rain
Why do you
Only come
When your heart's in pain?

/ roses /

The scent of roses makes me cry
How could something so beautiful
So lovely
Just wither away and happily die

/ gold /

Sometimes I wish I wasn't so broken
But maybe someday I could
Glue myself back together
With liquid gold

/ *heartsease* /

A random Wednesday
The streets glisten and reflect
The quiet moment it creates
For only today
Watching the occasional car *swoosh* by
Watching the world we share
A heartsease sigh

/ why did you stay /

Why did you not turn into
The beautiful flower you are
The sun was there
The rain showered love
But in the seed you stayed
Hugging the walls that kept you safe
Why did you stay?
The winter came, then spring again
By then you had no more hope
The warmth begged you to join the world
But in the seed you stayed

/ *if it never stops raining* /

Before the rain makes its way in
I pause and the world twinkles
From each raindrop as it sings
Clearing the day for tomorrow
If it never stops raining
I'll be okay

/ i'll erase everything at noon /

I'll erase everything at noon
Pretend like yesterday never happened
That yesterday
Was a figment of my imagination

Daydreaming at Noon

/ daydream /

I could be living in a daydream
I wouldn't even know
All the lights of colors
The happy little things
Like a drop of rain
Falling off a leaf
A beautiful song
Of a lonely bird
With nothing going on
I wouldn't even know
I could be living in a daydream
But when I open my eyes
I'm sitting by a tree
Looking up at the rain
Falling off a leaf

/ would i fly /

In dreams they told me not to live
But then
How would I fly?

/ stuck /

The life I hope
The dreams I dream
All the happy moments
It's all too sweet

/ *clipped wings* /

If birds could fly
I would take them with me
Over the clouds and streams
Dodging every breath
That they can't see
Oh, if only they could fly like me
I would show them the world
They've never seen

/ blue is just a color /

I've always admired how blue the sky was
It always kept its opinion to itself
Ignoring the rumors on how its color came to be
And when the grey clouds blocked its attention
It waited for the sun to give it back
Even northern blues couldn't help but wonder
Where the sky would ultimately end
Unnoticed, its humbleness remains
Letting the color blue
Remain his beloved name

/ somewhere /

Somewhere over the rainbow
I wanna sing with the blue birds too

/ days do go by faster /

Got my head in the clouds
And I'm not sure how to come down
Forever daydream living

/ *i miss* /

Oh how I miss
The trees dancing
Birds singing me memories
Clouds observing
And the mountains
Creating the stories
How I miss the simple things
That once made me happy

/ and for eternity /

Beautiful moments pass by too
Even though I wish they would *last forever*

/ pastime /

Painting the sky with clouds
My mind's favorite pastime

/ sky full of dreams /

Sitting on the roof
Pointing at the clouds
Drawing hearts and stars
For the ones who forgot

/ saddest moment /

The plucking of the strings
The gentle strum echoing
Every day the forest hums
Who could it be?
Sounds of joy gently in rhythm
And sometimes anger
Thumping the guitar rim
But a gloomy sound it is
When his sobs could be heard
Mumbling random words
Creating a depressing tune
And when the forest no longer
Hums, sings, or cries
In my heart
That's the saddest moment in life

/ to the moon /

I just want to lay in a field of tall flowers
And watch the stars blink my sadness away
All while they sing a lullaby to
The moon

/ dreams are supposed to be beautiful /

"This life is like a dream"

"A dream?"

"Although somehow it's
fake enough for wonderful
days, but real enough for
heartaches and pain"

/ dandelion /

Dandelion tufts bunched in my hand
Giving one to every person I meet
What a silly child I was
In the good I only believed

/ *little monsters* /

Over the hills of weary trees
Home to all the little monsters
Caring and kind, they're all looked after
Wistful and blissful, a world of laughter
They love their found home
Their happily forever after

/ *in a dream* /

The air smells of summer sweet
The world of color green
The rocky road in front of me
Sunflowers happily in a dream

/ finally found /

All I could think
Was to get away from my mind
To a place so beautiful
Where the sun never stops shining
And my smile, finally found

/ *birds* /

They sing
And the world spins slower

/ *smile, too* /

My, my, my
Why do you smile like that
When clouds blanket the sky
And the grass now brown
Or how the air is always grey?
Why? Can I ask, how?
Maybe knowing
Could help me
Feel as you do

/ bird with a purpose /

A view of the grassy meadow and beautiful light
You can't see, but I'm there
Sitting and counting each bird that lands
On the tree I decided to call on
Each bird with a purpose
More purpose than the sun

/ joyous world /

I want to be part of that world
The people controlled with kindness
An eternity of happiness
A place so hidden from the public eye
Getting there might never happen
A world that's created from the depths of dark
Into joyous redemption
A place that only truly lives
In our imagination

/ *hummingbird* /

A hummingbird in the light
So magical, yet
A flower out of sight

/ better places /

I learned to skip a rock
Across the glistening water
But I'd like to think
It's still moving on
To better places
Towards better things
Somehow
I'd like to think

/ *gentle tunes* /

Gentle tunes
While the ocean sings
Sunlight in a trance
Beautiful flowers it brings
Nothing could be more perfect
Than this beautiful blue-painted dream

/ too close to the sun /

I was too close to the sun, they said
And could burn my thoughts to a simmer
And all would be left is a silver smoke
Of glimmer

/ *little things* /

Sitting on the cloud
The world is much more beautiful
All the mistakes hidden
By all the glorious lights I see at night

/ *like stars in the sky* /

The world is upside down
I'm walking on clouds
And the city above
People glistening like stars

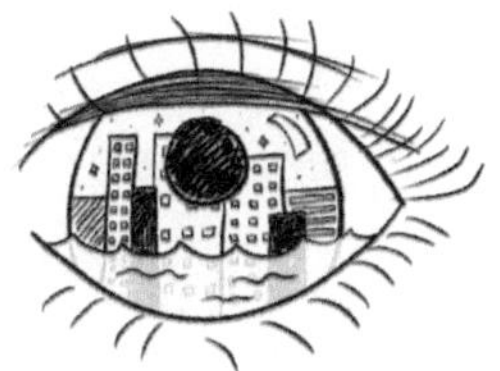

/ *imaginary things* /

All we do is stare through screens
Thinking of imaginary things

/ *lucky you* /

The stars crackled
Pieces flew to the earth
Finding them was the hard part
But lucky you
One fell into your hands
You never had to move too far

/ *the way stars sing* /

The way the stars sing
My heart yearns so
For them
Their echoes through the night sky
Reach out to grab my hand
Until they are close enough to hear
That's the way I dreamed
They would sing

/ conversations /

I love conversing with the stars
They don't have an ounce of judgment
In their souls

/ zoom in /

Zoom in with your camera
I can't see the sky

/ behind the stars /

Where can I find you?
I've looked over the mountains
Behind the stars, behind the stars
You don't want to be found
I raced through the oceans
And swam in the trees
But I cannot find you
Why is that?
If you could give me a hint
By lighting a candle so
I could find you
I will not take you back
Don't worry about that
The quiet world keeps moving past the skies
We will sit behind the light
Waiting for that one day
The world can find us
Behind the stars

/ *my sister once said* /

The skies have no business
Being this beautiful

/ *never ours* /

There is something magical
About wishing on a star
We wish with knowing
It may never become ours

/ *lonely one* /

The moon doesn't think anything of it
But it has no idea
How its ghostly light
Saved so many
Who feared the dark

/ valley of lights /

Valleys and valleys of lights
I can almost hear them humming
The cars singing
The people dreaming

/ *amongst the smiling clouds* /

Down the bike path
On this mountainside
Wind flowing through my hair
Purple skies

/ *change the world* /

It's enchanting to think
How one little idea of yours
Can change the world

/ *careless* /

Jumping
Skating through the streets
Meeting friends
By the oceanside
Endless words
Saying our first goodbyes

/ *last of us* /

The last of the umbrellas
Float to rise
Leaving me behind
To stroll with time

/ getting there /

Dreaming with my heart
Getting there with my mind

/ good days /

If I only had good days
I could see the world differently
I would be more happy
Every color a little brighter
And every person a little bit nicer
And bad days
Just a far bit lighter

/ cherry blossoms /

Falling
Waking up spring
Pink hearts covering my path
And when the wind gently blows
Flowers shower the air above
I'm in awe
And when the wind stops
I scoop them up and throw them back
Into the pink air I adore

/ hidden path of flowers /

On this path to where I go
Plant a flower here and here

/ tainted world /

Rose-colored glasses
Make my world
Just a little more idyllic

/ when the parakeets fly north /

When the parakeets fly north
Then we should worry
Their beautiful chirps become a blur
Almost forgotten
Every day
We wait outside
For their colors to appear
But when the world remains dull
It builds in us this fear
The seed that it will be forgotten
The love, the bliss
Will dissolve into the abyss
The sadness in us lifts
Hope is the only thing
The only thing that makes us wait
Another day, for spring

/ *his empty home* /

Nothing else mattered but
Giving her soul and putting it in our hands
Her memories she hid within the stars
For us to look up and remember
Her beautiful beautiful heart

/ *the distance from the earth to the stars* /

He saw this world all for them
In which he was forced to endure
A life of rigorous strength
Moving his town
In unconventional ways
Living for change
Not seeing much of a distance
Always flying back and forth
From the earth to the stars

/ *a good life* /

In the end we're all just visitors
In a thing called "life"

/ reach /

In this place we live
Love and hate surround us
A world so far away from us
And the hearts we care for
Just within our reach

/ *wishing today goodbye* /

Take my hand through the meadows
That twinkle towards the sky
The sun gently whistles
Wishing today goodbye

/ honey bear's comb /

So sweet like a honey bear's comb
You keep this world a gem

/ *she wonders* /

This little day
Wonders why
They leave her behind
So easily

/ only sight that's more /

The only sight that's more
Beautiful than the green summer
More lovely than pink tulips
And more sweet than lemonade
Is your honeydew face
On this glorious day

/ *my future prince* /

Every day, a genuine smile
So sweet and kind he makes honey melt
Confidence subtly radiates through
And he's twinkling with humbleness, too
I'm never his second choice, only first
And he is mine, for what it's worth
I'm sure he loves me
More than I could myself
And this broken heart, he'll always hold
My lovely future prince

/ love as a human /

She celebrates when you win
He comforts you when you cry
And when it all falls apart
They are there until you die
She hates when you feel mad
He cares when you beam
Even if you may not know it
They are never going to leave

/ *the edge* /

It's always hard to put
Into words how you think
All the seamless things
All the wondrous dreams
Clear your mindful streets
And if you squint far enough
Past the endless parade
You can see they are waiting
For you
At the edge for someday

/ *if i weren't me* /

I think a lot about who I would be
If I weren't me
If I were that stranger, staring at the red light
Or that guy walking his dog
Maybe that girl arguing with her friend
Or even that old calm woman
Sitting on the park bench
I wonder what their thoughts would be
How they would dream
Sometimes I wonder
If they ever thought
What if
They were me

/ a drive to the sun /

Driving on a glass road
Below is a world of buildings
People, cars
The road seems
To tilt upwards
Towards the sun
It almost feels like I'm flying
No twists, no turns
Below is a world of green and blue
I'm still driving, landing among the fog and blur
It's difficult to tell if
I'm falling
Or if this is all a simple turn
Breaking through
Below, a world of smiling clouds
I knew this was true

/ *continued memories* /

So many memories
That live forever as dreams

/ *road trip heaven* /

The sunlight moves through
Dancing through the windshield
Hand in the wind, I could almost steal it
Keeping it with me forever
The smell of lavender floats in the air
Putting me in a daydream
Thinking
Heaven couldn't be
More beautiful than this

/ *thunderstorm* /

They saw a thunderstorm
Only as simply aesthetic

/ how wonderful /

Sitting beneath a tree
Admiring
How wonderful it grew to be

Realizing Me

/ *this is for happiness* /

What if I don't make it in time?
The road I'm walking on
Could take too long
Even if I run, or bike, or drive
It just might be too far
With oblivion only in front of me
I've decided regret is worse
I've decided the only way
For me to perceive happiness
In this underrated universe
Is to lead myself forward
A beautiful journey
Never unheard

/ *living* /

Only I can comprehend
How much I mean to me

/ *beyond the stars* /

I don't want to settle for ordinary
Since everything I want to achieve
Is sitting just beyond the stars

/ chasing fireflies /

Like a stranger I saw myself
All the dreams I could've been
I let me down
The clouds disappeared beneath my feet
And noticed I fell
I reached above the sky to catch the moon
Someone else was there
Better than me they were
Younger than me
All the dreams I wanted to be
I can't stop though
Chasing fireflies in the sky
"I have to be great" I tell myself
It's the only way to fly

/ save myself /

I have to save myself
So when I finally find the true meaning
Of being me
Then
I can find someone
Who needs saving too

/ *little dreams* /

I always thought of them as little dreams
Until I closed my eyes for days
Where many became a lovely reality

/ start /

If I could get there, I would
The goals I crave, I could
The diminished fate
Too lost
Maybe one day
I'll start

/ still i wanted to be /

They said I had to choose
My dream
But there was so much
I still wanted to be

/ found myself /

I was never good at finding things
But somehow
I kindly found myself
And somehow
I feel as if I'm still looking

/ *trying to escape* /

In a maze of trees
Which way do I go?
Every tree says
"You haven't seen me before"
No one there
To point me in the right direction
This haunting time I've spent
Running in circles
Could've been saved
Had I remembered to wait
Had I remembered to see
The lovely birds hidden in the trees
Understanding what difference
They could make to this dream
Instead of trying to escape
What I thought I needed to believe

/ tightrope /

Just once, I look back
Seeing who I was told to leave behind
Sense a tear forming
Watching as it fell with the rain
Should I turn back?
Or continue
Reaching for my other hand
That's waiting

/ endlessly /

Hardships are endless
I'm struggling now, but maybe one day I'll
Be stronger than endless too

/ my dad once told me /

Fear is the devil

/ *time* /

Fearless, she decides to rise
Against herself, against the time
Placing her heart for the ones she loves most
Deciding her life should not be for nothing
Although time is now an enemy
She'll try to make it her friend
Because fighting with it after all these years
Time is who she needs forgiveness from

/ *empty promises* /

Empty promises I make every day
Not for you, but for me
The more promises I make
The less I'm able to keep

/ *today* /

I wanted to hate you
But I couldn't
Why couldn't you
Do as you promised?
Is life a game?
I understand your pain
And time has to heal your wounds
But stop saying tomorrow
I will do what I have to do
But I could never hate you
Because you are someday
Going to be someone
Important to me, someone
Who got to their dreams, someone
Despite the ultimate rainy days
Could pick out her favorite star
And know what I didn't know yesterday
I know today how important
You were to me

/ you will be first /

My darling, I'll put you on hold
Until the day I can put you first
When you don't have to be last anymore
The day will come, I hope
Because my eyes lighten
When I see you happy
Although those times are not enough
Someday I'll put you first

/ waits for no one /

Thinking of the sun
Who waits for no one
Oblivious to what they say
For how it must be hidden
In a world like today

/ break /

The people with the biggest hearts
Seem to always be
The first ones to break

/ i'm okay with me /

Stars shine when they talk
Northern lights cry when they smile
Flowers grow where they walk
I wanted to be them

/ *change* /

Breaking the voices
Changing the rules
What you think you know now
That will change too

/ *meteoroid* /

Sometimes I wonder
If the stars aren't meant to be mine
I wonder
If I'm supposed to be a meteoroid
Just floating on by
In the background of the great galaxy
Living in silence
But I don't want to be forgotten
Even if I'm a rock floating in no direction
Someday they'll see a comet
With their reflection

/ be /

Everyone's living in a fantasy
Where the clouds hover below our knees
Blue lights cover the skies
I just want to be
Cities hiding for the night
No one in sight
Here
I just want to be

/ *maybe one day* /

Maybe one day
I'll see the world for what it is
Maybe one day
It'll love me back again

/ the night falls /

The darkness is my friend
It wasn't at first, but then I realized
Stars only exist in the dark
And I exist in the stars

/ your heart /

If I asked you what matters most
You'll consider everything
All the people you know
The things you've hoped for
Ignorant to the one
The heart of it all
Who stood by your side
Never asking you for more

/ *myself and i* /

My little friend
Why was I so mean?
I told you
You were weak
I told you
You can't reach your dream
And when you started to cry
I told you to keep it inside
You never listened to me though
And it angered me
I knew how hurt you would be
To not make that one in a billion dream
As you grew, you taught me
What my stubborn mind didn't know
And I knew how wrong
I was
For trying to keep me
Safe all along

/ and still it remains there /

When I never found my gold
I planted a flower
Where I figured
I left my lonely heart

/ *distant thoughts* /

Can I take this any longer?
The minute, the second, the hour?
If I had known, I would have never come
If I had only known
How I would be alone
I thought I wanted to be here
Soaring among the stars
But now I see I'm just floating
With no one by my heart
Was all the hype worth it
If I have to live like this
Every minute, every second, every hour
Oh, then I would miss
The distant thoughts
Of my future bliss

/ growing thorns /

When pushed to their limits
Even cherry blossoms
Can learn to grow thorns

/ *shadow* /

My shadow gently held my hand
Guiding me home
To my forgotten heart

/ *this moment in time* /

The lights that cover my eyes
Blind me in this moment in time
The feeling of joy
The feeling of calmness
As well the feeling of something missing
I don't know where to find
The lights that blind me
The lights that are supposed to guide me
Are just a happy illusion they tell you to believe
Stepping into the darkness, into nothingness
Looking for your light in the distance
In this moment
That finally
Allows me to see

/ *missing me* /

Remember when I used to smile
With chubby cheeks and a pearly tooth
My light wheat hair on my soft head
Or the darkness that souled in my youth
When I took my first stomp
Your eyes sparked in unison
And when I said my first word
Nothing was more important then
Oh, how I miss to be this young
Without a worry or care
Letting bigger ones decide my way
Like a baby bear
And letting them always know
When I wanted to play
Because after all that
I learned to find my way

/ see herself /

She did once see herself
Just as they wanted her to be
Until one day
Her heart grew bigger
Than their words

/ stars shined /

Why did I think
The world wasn't for me
That the stars couldn't shine for me
That the grass beneath my shoes
Were meant for everyone but me
But I think I know now
Now I think I know
It might be too late
But I hope I'm wrong
And other times I think
That the stars shined
Exactly in the moment
They wanted me to smile
That the stars have always shined
I just couldn't see
So why did I have to think
That the world
Wasn't for me

/ who you are /

I couldn't be someone *you* wanted me to be
Instead became someone *I* wanted to see

/ until the next one /

It's okay to hurt
Sit yourself down and breathe
Trickled tears shouldn't hold you back
The words you want to speak
Put your mind together with glue
Sometimes one won't want to stay
Just sit yourself down and place it back
Gently with care, time can wait

/ piece by piece /

Putting yourself together
Stem by stem
Flower by flower

/ from a distance /

You think I'm a failure
That my life isn't put together
How the stars have all
Flown away from me
Making you think you're better than me
But after a moment of sitting
With my knuckles under my chin
I watch the orange sunset in the distance
Listening to the words under my skin
I may have been slower
I may have been too sensitive
I may have been working too much
For nothing
But I will prove to you
That I can reach it, and if I don't
If the stars never return
Then at least I know
I'll always see the them
Past the sunset in the distance

/ not just yet /

What's this life about
When do I learn how to grow up
But not just yet
Because I want to play in the meadows
Swing from the clouds
Draw little smiles on every frown
Not just yet, because you see
I want to sing my heart out
From the top of the earth
Hug every cat that crosses my path
And keep every flower I search for
And in my backpack with pink hearts
It's where I keep my soul
So when I'm lost
I'll know what life
Was all about before

/ subconscious /

Because if a memory is gone
It's always easy to let go

/ *blinded* /

Stepping into the sun
I'm happily blinded
By the way the sun sings

/ what makes me stand out /

Entirely nothing
And yet everything

/ *moving shadows* /

Shadows move across the room
Living through this glorious day
Until the sun hides its face again

/ *silent poems* /

It is my dream, but why do I fear it so
Is it the people that might criticize my work
Or is it the failure I don't want to set for myself?
No one even knows, I hide it so well
Where my heart is, they can't tell
Once I break that barrier and let them read
All the silent poems they wouldn't believe

/ *okay* /

If I grow up, stop being young
I might not be me anymore
But I won't know until the time comes
When I do have to grow
And be someone I've never met before
Someone who sees the world a little deeper
And the skies a little bit farther
If I grow up and stop being younger
I could be wiser
Maybe, just maybe
I'll be okay

/ the day i dream of /

The sweet sound of my alarm
Brightens the world
Softly pulling the curtains away
To let the sun be my friend again
I'm not late today so I can stop
And stare into the ocean
Knowing that, I let myself dance
Into the day I've always dreamed of

/ running /

I'm running
And ready to fly

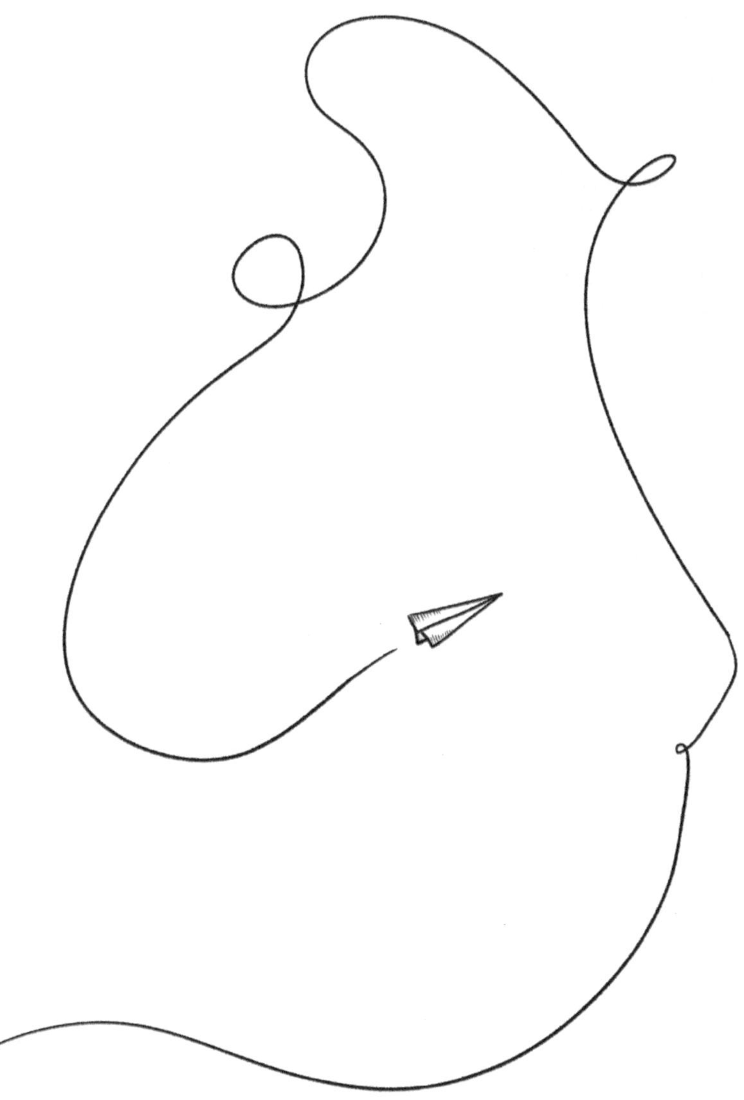

/ happy me /

Spinning across the floor
My floating hair
Gently falling
Gentle tunes
Swirling in the air
And when I stop
In the window I see
The reflection of my happy me

/ broken me /

Broken me
I learned so much
From you

/ believe in my dreams, believe in me /

You always work hard for what you want
And someday you'll get there
I promise
Every morning, you fix your early heart
Before starting your day
So you can someday rise up to the stars
And tell yourself
"I believed in you this way"

/ always home /

My soul's most precious home
My heart

/ my little me /

Like a child, I convince myself
Sometimes I rebel
Other times, I forcefully listen
I haven't taught myself
To happily win
But as I grow older and become wiser
I hope to have raised this girl
To embrace her hidden confidence
Cherish her intelligent mind
And to give herself the love
She's forgotten to revise
With a little kindness and time
I hope she sees
How much I've always loved her
My little me

/ you /

Love yourself more than your dreams
Because *you* are your biggest dream

/ nothing more powerful /

Nothing is as powerful
As that day
You found yourself enough

/ *let me walk* /

Let me walk my path
So let me start
I know this journey will
Break me, but I know
It will also make me
Into someone
I've always dreamed
Who's found their heart
In this forgotten reality

/ your worth /

Your worth is soaring
Through your veins

Sara Hajipouri

Finding You

/ *someone else* /

You've never been to the beach
You've never seen the moon
The touch of the wind
Has never been yours
A little flower in this winter storm
You want to fit in
But still, you can't make it to the top
Only then
When the mountain is still
It takes all your might to finally
Trust you can only be yourself

/ *a million and one* /

Our eyes hold a million memories

/ so dearly /

A daisy on my front porch
From nowhere I could tell
Yellow petals faded to brown
Green stem sadly drowned
I thought long about its journey here
How it came to me so dear
Even with its imperfections so clear
I loved it so dear
But how sad it looked alone on this porch
Away from the other daisies
Away from its home

/ yours /

So many broken hearts in the world
And I only see yours

/ when you loved yourself /

With all the world's pain
Bringing you down
It's easy to forget
When you loved yourself

/ cry for you /

I shouldn't have to cry for you
Because
If they cherished you
If they ever loved you
Then
I wouldn't have to cry for you

/ why don't you see /

The beauty in your heart
Is completely relevant too

/ souls are starting to cry /

I get sad when I think of you
Because the soul you once treasured
The world took for granted

/ in my heart you'll stay /

I keep angels beside me
Close by
Because the one time I didn't
They flew away
And never came back

/ wishing on flowers /

You make wishing on flowers and dreams
A beautiful thing

/ endless thinking /

All the hints you didn't see
Were silently killing me

/ fall back to earth /

Only I can be there
For you
But you don't know
All the times
I gave up my time
To miss the sunsets
How I cried for you
Instead of laughing with friends
All the times
I waited
For you to fall back to earth
And still I waited
And still I'll wait

/ what if... /

What if I could
Write your name in the stars
Would you then be able to finally
See your worth

/ *you cross their minds* /

Listening and waiting too long
Forgetting you once crossed their minds

/ *hate eventually rots flowers* /

"I hate this world"

"Please don't…"

"Why not? It was never nice
to me"

"Because it's not about how
nice they are or aren't. If
you carry hate in your
heart, you'll turn out exactly
like them"

/ never held you back /

As kind as you are
I wish it never held you back

/ broken wings are sometimes perfect /

Angels fall sometimes
But you know what
Broken wings are much more beautiful
Than perfect

/ broken wings are sometimes perfect /

/ honeybees /

I will take your worries
Put them in a jar
Sing them a lullaby
Every night
I'll raise them for you
Until they are grown
Finally understanding
Where your mind was at that time
And when they are ready to fly
Like honeybees
We'll let them pass us by

/ this time, time waits for you /

That's okay
If your heart befriends time
To heal

/ *before we fade again* /

All the calls started fading
Little by little, we became strangers
And if I saw you today, I wouldn't know you
You'd be another person in the crowd
That's the way it goes
And if we pretend like everything is good
Maybe if, by chance, we meet
It won't take too long
Before we learn to laugh again

/ collecting stars /

I hate how it took me this long
I'm here now
Handing you every star I have
Every star I've counted in your name

/ don't you ever worry /

If only I had known when
Your laughter turned to silence
The spark in your eyes
Turned to stone
And the world from your view
Meant nothing more
I would've been there sooner
Helping you see the world
Just a little bit brighter
Just a little bit kinder
In this place, you're longing for home
I'm by your side now
Don't you worry
I may have been engulfed
In my own problems, I'm sorry
But I'm by your side now
Don't you ever worry

/ they're closer than you think /

How long has it been
Since I first saw your dreams bloom
I wish spring
Wasn't so far away from you

/ go /

In a blink, I can go
Desperate hands can hold me back
But in a blink, I will go
Do not mourn me, flower friend
All the stars were on my path
So, goodbye to the world
That grew me old
In a blink, I faintly go

/ people and promises /

"I'm going to miss this place"

"You don't have to miss it. You
don't have to go…"

"I'd like to think I have control…
but I don't. Life doesn't work like
that. I won't be gone long. I
promise I'll be back someday and
just like old friends do, we'll live
as if we're kids again, just for
one day"

You promised…"Okay…someday"

/ kind sadness /

I'm in need of your kind words
Tell me that it will be okay
Tell me that what sadness you have
Will be here only for today

/ twinkle in your eye /

A twinkle in your eye
A freckle on your nose
A slightly raised eyebrow
You couldn't believe them
Their broken-tiled words

/ *turning away* /

Broken mirrors
Sideways stares
Turning away
Because you dared

/ speckled eyes /

Glitter speckles your eyes in a way you don't expect
Torn by the wonders of making dreams come true
Broken by the way they never do
Flying to a place so they can understand
Tyrant voices swallow your truth
Never finding a place that comprehends
Creating one that does in time
By the wonders of making dreams come true
The way glitter speckles in your eyes

/ *just by chance* /

You're slowly getting to shine
Just like the stars you don't yet see at night
Brilliance takes time

/ enough for me /

"You have to know that
there're people who
care about you"

"Who?…You're the
only one"

"Am I not enough?"

/ i'll give the world to you /

You deserve the world
But you'll never know it

/ *saturn's rings* /

Sitting on Saturn's rings
I knew you were on the opposite side
Looking up, admiring the brightest star
It flickered out of sight
Knowing only you
Would make it disappear
Making room among the stars
For someone else just as bright
Just as you are, my dear

/ dazzling mind /

Give me your dazzling mind
So I can do what you do
It's hard for me to say
How much I envy you

/ don't miss me /

Your heart so pure
Even the lights couldn't blind you
But don't miss me sky nova
Keep the light in your eyes
Don't leave your heart
Aching
For moving on with my life

/ *let us dream* /

The world isn't so big
We'll see each other again
A comet in the sky
And my heart within

/ *few others* /

By the way, I never told you lies
I treated everyone to their own devise
Those who glared at me with hate
Those who thought I was nothing
More than a pretty flower
Then there were those I loved
Who put me first before the world
So I could once fly again

/ change yourself /

On the bus stop
I see you there
Walking on air
Somehow you've changed
For the better
As the city bus comes near
Hesitation arises
Because you fear
What they say
But
You've changed
For the better
Their minds
Still walking on air

BUS
STOP

/ we all miss you /

I do miss you, but I won't say
Although my tears might speak otherwise
But please ignore them
Because I haven't figured out yet
That all good things will someday return
And I won't miss you anymore
When you're finally here standing in front of me
Waving only from a distance

/ *good night* /

I do wish you a gentle good night
And leave all your worries for yesterday

/ promise me /

I don't ever ask anything from you
But promise me
You'll be happy
That's all I want
That's all I want from you

/ to you /

The floor like glass
With the sunset shining through
I can't tell
Where is the beginning or end
It doesn't bother me
Since I know
I'm walking to you

/ raining flowers /

I wish it rained flowers
Every day, so that every day
Could remind me of you

/ *magic* /

And as the magic of happiness sets in
All the little sad moments you'd seen
Someday covered with a path
Of your flowers and memories

/ *my light* /

I can only see the light behind you
You're smiling but I can't see
You're reaching but I can't see
It's calling for you again but please
Don't go, don't leave me
This place is not the same
Let me go with you but I know I can't
I'll have to wait
But you can see my light
That I didn't see
Shining even brighter behind me

/ are you okay /

Smile a little bit wider
It's the only expression I know
To see that you are doing well

/ from the sky for you /

I'll tie a bow on this star
I plucked from the sky for you
Put it on your doorstep
And watch you follow your dreams

/ fire flowers /

It might be a little difficult
It might take some time
But as you're reaching
For your goal
Your dream
I'll cheer you on
From the sidelines
Because I knew
That spark in your soul
That spark in your heart
Once so small
Is now blooming fire
Flowers for the world

/ hearts /

I did forget to mention
How the world lights
For you
How they smile
Just for you

/ *please don't leave* /

"I never knew"

"You never knew what?"

"I never knew just how
bright the stars shine
when you're here"

/ *please don't leave* /

/ *every year* /

Every year I wait
For the sun to circle you again

/ *success* /

Give me your mind
Give me your dreams
You make it so easy
To succeed

/ green leaf /

Are you waiting by the tree
Where I found you three years ago
Near the little stone I told myself not to throw
Or did you decide to move across the water
Where I wouldn't be able to find your heart
Like a kind game of hide and seek
I hope that you are still there
It would make me so happy
If you're somehow still there
Waiting for me

/ my someone's wish /

Clasping your hands together
To make a wish
Like a dolphin you see the world
For what it is
The wrinkles when you scrunch your nose
Is nothing a cat can compare
And when your eyes open with grace
A vibrant green angel would stare
With the swift air of a hummingbird's wing
The light is dismissed
And the way you linger your gaze
Proves to all that I was your wish

/ yellow words /

Your yellow words circle my brain
Your happiness engraved
Every chance I want to see
Your words smiling back at me
Every time I close my eyes
I'm lost in this moment in time

/ *best friend* /

You're my best friend
I'll take you by the hand
And we'll sit in clouds
Share our worries and dreams
A moment away from reality

/ *pretty* /

I love the word pretty
It describes your soul
And your views
And your lovely words, too

/ *that one rainy day* /

The sun shines today
But all I can think about
Is that one rainy day
Where we jumped in puddles
And how we smiled
With our faces towards the thunder

/ *smiling face* /

The day I met you is a blur
A smiling face you always had
I brushed your hair
To keep seeing you happy
And made you soup
On cold summer days
The advice I gave was only said
For you to be great
The swings I pushed
So you could fly
Interests change as time strikes
I try to wave goodbye
Still you have that smiling face
Every time you run to me
I know I'm alright

/ *shining light* /

You are more than just my shining light
You are all the stars
A beautiful altruistic mind

/ *i can't forgive you* /

You wish I could forgive you
For all the things
For making me feel that
I don't need anyone else but me
For teaching me how to
See the beauty in this ugly world
For staying by my side
When I thought I would fall
For giving me all the love you had
To raise me as the kindest soul
So no
I can't forgive you
When there is nothing
To forgive at all

/ if only you knew /

What made you think your dreams
Couldn't become reality?

/ *blooming* /

A blossom blooming
In a volcanous storm
Is strength even
You didn't know you had

/ beautiful things /

At an early age
I deemed myself unsmart
Part of the cosmos
And they were the stars
So practical, so logical
The world outside found their worth
And not mine
Because I dreamed, because I imagined
Beautiful things
So far from the ground
My head gleamed to be
At an early age
I didn't know
That the world outside doesn't see
Each living person
And their cherished dreams
In this illusion of reality
At an early age
I believed myself smart
Part of the cosmos
And among them
I, too, was a star

/ fighting blindly /

Your heart doesn't see
If you made it
To your dreams
Fighting blindly
Keeping you alive
Knowing this fight
Was not a waste of time

/ well past mars /

Just go towards that dream
You've got one life, one shot
To live it well past
Just the moon and stars

/ *letter to myself* /

I want you to feel beautiful
To feel strong
To feel that a rocket
Couldn't even stop your launch
Of who you want to be
Those that dare to dream
I want you to feel
You can be anything

/ lovely as a flower /

Everyone needs a friend
As lovely as a flower

FLOWER FRIEND
INDEX

256... honeybees
258... this time, time waits for you
259... before we fade again
260... collecting stars
261... don't you ever worry
262... they're closer than you think
263... go
264... people and promises
265... kind sadness
266... twinkle in your eye
267... turning away
268... speckled eyes
269... just by chance
270... enough for me
271... i'll give the world to you
272... saturn's rings
274... dazzling mind
275... don't miss me
276... let us dream
277... few others
278... change yourself
280... we all miss you
281... good night
282... promise me
283... to you
284... raining flowers
286... magic
287... my light
288... are you okay
289... from the sky for you
290... fire flowers
292... hearts
293... please don't leave
294... every year
295... success
296... green leaf
297... my someone's wish
298... yellow words
299... best friend
300... pretty
301... that one rainy day
302... smiling face
303... shining light
304... i can't forgive you
305... if only you knew
306... blooming
308... beautiful things
310... fighting blindly
311... well past mars
312... letter to myself
313... lovely as a flower

ACKNOWLEDGMENTS

Baba (Hassan Hajipouri), I want to thank you for all the years of support and for never having an ounce of doubt towards me and my goals, even when I doubted myself. None of this book, my dreams, would ever be possible without you. I want you to know that you're the reason I am able to reach for the moon and stars. You truly are the best father anyone could ever ask for.

Shakiba Hajipouri, I thank you, my sister, for being the editor for my debut book. You took time out of your days to help because you believed in me, and I will always appreciate you. I wish you to achieve anything your heart desires.

Nuran Hajipouri, thank you little sister for being a glimmer of sunshine throughout the time I stressed out about the publishing process for this book and for always reminding me to work on my dreams.

My readers, I want to thank you. As much as I write for myself, I write for you. Your everlasting support and encouragement have brought me to where I am today, and you have truly shown me that I'm never alone throughout my writing journey. Always remember the value of your own journey as well. You are important too.

ABOUT THE AUTHOR

Sara Hajipouri, originally born in Kurdistan, embarked on a journey to the United States alongside her family when she was just three years old. Even before she realized her passion for writing, Sara had been immersed in the world of classic children's poetry from Kurdistan, courtesy of her father who often gifted her poetry books. Throughout her school years, she found herself drawn towards writing and art classes, participating in small competitions without fully realizing the direction her passion was pulling her towards.

In 2020, Sara earned a degree in Business Administration and Management from Minnesota State University Moorhead. While owning a business had also been an accomplished and cherished dream of hers, Sara had a strong feeling towards forging meaningful connections through the idea of words. She believes her poetry can one day provide support to others, just as they have comforted her continually.

Beyond her writing endeavors, Sara gains joy in discovering new music, watching movies, creating art, crafting stories, spending time among nature, and forming lasting memories. Her two cats and sheep hold special places in her heart. Her family, friends, and the moments spent with them, are what she cherishes most of all.

In 2023, Sara accomplished a significant milestone with the release of her debut poetry collection, titled *Flower Friend*, with plans to unveil a special edition in the near future. The book is a testament to her artistic journey, in which she hopes to touch the lives of others, just as her own life has been positively impacted by the power of words.

Sara Hajipouri

www.sarahajipouri.com